THE SEVEN RAVENS

A story by the Brothers Grimm
with pictures by Felix Hoffmann

Harcourt, Brace & World, Inc., New York

For Dieter

Once upon a time there was a man who had seven sons,

but, much as he loved them,
he longed for a daughter.

At last his wife told him they were to have another child, and when it was born, it was a girl. The man and his wife were delighted, but the child was weak and small, and they were afraid she would not live long. So they decided to have her baptized at once and sent one of the boys to fetch water from the well.

The other six went with him.
Each wanted to draw the water,
and in the struggle
the jug fell and was smashed.

They stood there,
not knowing what to do,
and none of them
dared to go home.

When they still did not return,
their father grew impatient and said:
"Those naughty boys must be
playing one of their games and
have forgotten about the water."
Then he grew very angry and shouted:
"I wish those wicked boys would
all be turned into ravens!"

No sooner had he spoken than
he heard a beating of wings
in the air above and,
looking up, saw seven
black ravens flying away.

The man and his wife were very sad to
lose their seven sons, but it was too late
to take back the curse. They found comfort
in their little daughter, who grew stronger
and more beautiful as each day went by.
For a long time she did not know that she
had ever had any brothers. Then one day
she heard some people say it was her
fault that her seven brothers had suffered
such cruel misfortune. So she went to
her parents and asked if it was true
that she had had seven brothers, and what
had become of them? The man and his wife
could keep the secret from her no longer,
so they told her how her brothers
had been changed into ravens.

Day by day the girl grew sadder.

Finally, she made up her mind to find her brothers and set them free.

She set out, taking with her nothing but a little ring that her parents

gave her, a loaf of bread in case she was hungry, a little bottle of water
in case she was thirsty, and a little chair in case she was tired.

She walked and walked, on and on, until she came to the end of the world,
but she found no trace of her brothers.

Then she came to the Sun,
but it was too hot and bright and
no little children lived there.

Quickly, she ran away and went to the Moon,
but it was too cold, and surly and bad-tempered
as well. When it saw her, it said: "Go away!
Go away!" She fled swiftly and came

to the stars, who were friendly
and kind to her, each one sitting
on its own special stool.
The morning star rose, gave her
a magic bone, and said: "You
will find your brothers inside the
Glass Mountain. But you cannot
open the Glass Mountain without
this magic bone."

The girl took the magic bone, wrapped it carefully in a piece of cloth, and went on her way until she reached the Glass Mountain. The door into it was shut. She opened the cloth to take out the bone, but the cloth was empty. She had lost the magic gift of the star. What could she do now? She must rescue her brothers, but she had no key to the Glass Mountain. Quickly she took a knife, cut off her little finger, stuck it into the lock, and the door opened.

When she had gone inside, a dwarf came
towards her and asked what she wanted.
"I am looking for my brothers, the seven ravens,"
she replied. The ravens were not at home, the
dwarf told her, but she could wait for them if she
liked. The girl watched him as he brought in
food and drink for the ravens, on seven little
plates and in seven little goblets.
From each plate she took a bite to eat,

and from each goblet she took a sip to drink,
and into the last goblet she dropped the
ring her parents had given her. At once she
heard a sighing sound in the air and a
beating of wings, and the dwarf said:
"The ravens are flying home."

The ravens arrived and looked
for their plates and goblets,
for they were hungry and thirsty.
Then, one after the other, they said:
"Who has eaten from my plate?
Who has drunk from my goblet?"
As the seventh raven emptied his
goblet, out rolled the ring.
He looked at it, and he knew it
was the ring that belonged to
his father and mother. "If only
our sister were here, then the
curse would be broken and we
should be set free," he said.
When the girl, who was standing
behind the door, heard his wish,

she stepped forward, and at once

the ravens were changed back

into her seven brothers.

They were overjoyed to see their

sister and to be free at last.

And they all went joyfully home together.